W9-AON-641

Five Little Monkeys Sitting in a Tree

EILEEN CHRISTELOW

sandpiper

Houghton Mifflin Harcourt

Boston   New York

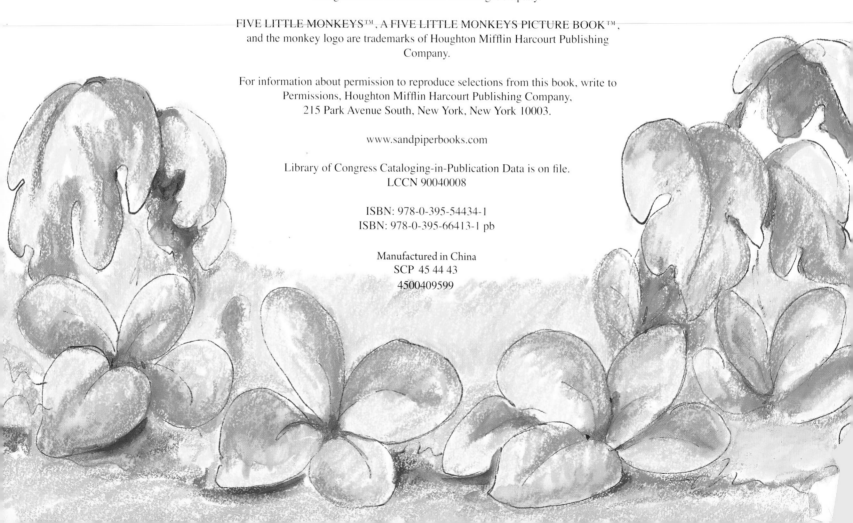

For a new batch of little monkeys—
Gregory, Sebastian, Nicole, Julia, and Olivia.

www.sandpiperbooks.com

Library of Congress Cataloging-in-Publication Data is on file.
LCCN 90040008

ISBN: 978-0-395-54434-1
ISBN: 978-0-395-66413-1 pb

Manufactured in China
SCP 45 44 43
4500409599

Five little monkeys and their mama
walk down to the river for a picnic supper.

Mama spreads out a blanket
and settles down for a snooze . . .

. . . while five little monkeys
climb a tree to watch Mr. Crocodile.

Five little monkeys, sitting in a tree,
tease Mr. Crocodile, "Can't catch me!"

Along comes Mr. Crocodile . . .

Oh, no! Where is she?

Four little monkeys, sitting in a tree,
tease Mr. Crocodile, "Can't catch me!"
Along comes Mr. Crocodile . . .

11

Oh, no! Where is he?

Three little monkeys, sitting in a tree,
tease Mr. Crocodile, "Can't catch me!"
Along comes Mr. Crocodile . . .

15

Oh, no! Where is he?

Two little monkeys, sitting in a tree,
tease Mr. Crocodile, "Can't catch me!"
Along comes Mr. Crocodile . . .

Oh, no! Where is she?

Now there's only one little
monkey, sitting in the tree,
teasing Mr. Crocodile,
"Can't catch me!"
Along comes Mr. Crocodile . . .

SNAP!

Oh, no! There are no little monkeys sitting in the tree. But, wait! Look!

1 2 3 4 5

Five little monkeys, sitting in the tree!

Their mama hugs them.

Their mama scolds them.
"Never tease a crocodile.
It's not nice—and it's dangerous."

Then five little monkeys and their mama
eat a delicious picnic supper.

And they do not tease Mr. Crocodile again!